STAGECOACH TO BREMER'S ROCK

A Jesse Garnett Western

R. Annan

One Vision Publishing

Stagecoach to Bremer's Rock
Copyright 2017 by R. Annan
WGA Reg. #: R32142 (1/30/217)

Author's Portrait: Hazel Tertsakian
Editor: Karren Doll Tolliver
Photography © L. Annan

One Vision Publishing
Published 2017

ISBN: 978-1-942338-70-3 (eBook)
ISBN: 978-1-942338-69-7 (Print)

Western books by R. Annan

Fight for the Lazy M
The Red Bandana
The Salvation of Trace Logan
The Cowboy from Sierra Blanca

Jack Cordell Westerns

The Gunfighter in Winter
Long Ride to Hell's Kitchen
Owl Hawks
Gunfight at Barfield Springs
Shootout at Sanctuary City
Last Days of a Gunfighter

Clay Jared Westerns

Copperhead Moon
Cowboys of the Box R
Prisoners of Brimstone Pass
Range War in C Minor
Devil Wind
Showdown at Wamego Falls
Lightning Riders
Winter Kill
Wild River
Shootout at Rattlesnake Flats

Jesse Garnett Westerns

Gunfight at Black Wolf Lair
Gunfight at Latigo Junction
Outcasts of Troublesome Creek
Stagecoach to Bremer's Rock

Dedication

To Lovers of God's Green Earth

Chapter 1

Winter wasn't far off. The leaves of the birches, aspens and scrub oaks were being snatched up by the winds and sent swirling and dancing over the ground, sparkling like colored jewels in the sunlight. The prairie grass was brown and bent over. The only green to be found was in the pines, in the juniper bushes and high in the hawthorn trees where emerald colored clusters of witches' broom clung to the top branches.

On a high ridge, a stag stood framed against a cold, blue sky. It watched as a four horse stagecoach crawled along the Ellis to Sterling coach road far below. Two other horses were tied to the back boot ramp. One was a chestnut mustang and the other was a black and white appaloosa.

A man in the coach happened to see the stag in the distance. He drew his Colt, stuck it out the window and thumbed off a single shot. The bullet landed short, but the echoing roar of the gun sent the noble beast plunging away into a stand of tall whispering pines. It was soon out of sight behind the ridgeline. The stagecoach rattled on.

"You missed!" a man in a city suit sitting next to the opposite window remarked sarcastically. He was a carpetbagger on his way to Ellis to sell his latest innovation, a can opener with an India rubber covered handle. It was made specifically to give a better grip, thus making it easier for housewives to open cans of fruit, vegetables, and lard.

"I was only trying to spook him," the man said. He smiled as he slowly eased his gun back in its holster.

He was a handsome man with black hair, large, dark eyes and a neatly trimmed black mustache. The brown suit he wore looked expensive. It suggested he was a gambler or a businessman. He might even possibly be a gunman. It was difficult to tell which. His hat was also black and matched the color of his boots. When he took out a deck of cards and toyed with it, that settled the question in the other passenger's minds. He was, no doubt, a gambler.

The man relaxed against the back wall of the coach and played with the cards. He smiled across at the woman sitting on the forward bench to the carpetbagger's left. She smiled back. He had noticed she was not wearing a ring, and he wondered how he might introduce himself to her. Her blue eyes and pale beauty held his attention and made it hard for him to look away. She didn't seem to resent his attention and sometimes favored him with a smile of her own.

The man sitting on her left was a pastor, which made three on her side. The pastor stared across at the man sitting next to the gambler. He was slumped down on the bench with his hat over his eyes. His worn, dog-eared suit, unkempt looks and unshaven face clearly marked him as a drifter, one of those poor souls afloat on the sea of humanity who had not yet found a safe harbor. He was clearly a sinner who needed redeeming. Just one week with the pastor and this lost soul would be healed again. The pastor was certain of that. A second thought entered the pastor's mind. Perhaps the man was an outlaw, a stage robber. The clergyman suddenly felt exposed and nervous.

The stagecoach hit a rut in the road and everyone lurched about. After that jolt, a cross wind blew a cloud of reddish dust inside the coach. The passengers coughed and rubbed their eyes. Those who had handkerchiefs covered their faces.

The driver, usually called a whip because he wielded one, yelled down to them. "Sorry about that bump, folks!" He cracked his rawhide whip and yelled at the horses.

It was getting colder now. The passengers pulled their coat collars higher and tighter to keep out the wind that crept through the cracks and crevices of the coach. They lowered the canvas window shades, but that didn't help much. The shades only flapped and rattled annoyingly in the wind and served no purpose.

At a speed of about seven miles an hour, it was a tedious ride. The long climb up hills, and the twists and turns in the road, seemed put there to make their lives a living hell. On the down side of the steep hills, the shotgun, the whip's assistant and guard, had to lower a heavy log to create a drag to check the speed of the coach. The brakes would scream, overheat and give off a horrible stench.

It was late afternoon when they rolled into Ralston's Gulch, their first stop on the way to Ellis, a hundred and thirty-five miles northwest. Sterling, their starting point, was a mere twenty-five miles behind them. Some of them still had a long way yet to go.

Ralston's Gulch was nothing but a solitary sod hut used as a quick stop. No one got off or on at this lonely place, but the horses were given grain, water, and a chance to rest. The attendants were an old man and his wife.

"Jesus!" the carpetbagger said. "They live way out here by themselves?"

The pastor crossed himself at the flippant use of the Lord's name. In half an hour, they were back on the road again.

"Are you alright, ma'am?" the gambler asked the lady.

She smiled at him and said, "Yes, thank you. I'm just a little cold."

He smiled back, trying to think of something to say to comfort her. He couldn't come up with any fancy words, so he just nodded and gave her a sympathetic look.

Nothing was said after that so they all settled down to endure the shaking and rattling of the coach. Time dragged on. The man in the dog-eared suit, who had been dozing throughout this ordeal, snorted and mumbled something. He leaned over against the gambler. The gambler shoved him roughly back into his corner by the opposite window. The man suddenly sat up and rubbed his eyes. He gazed around the coach with a dazed look on his face.

"Are we there?" he asked, scratching his stubbly chin and sniffing.

They all started laughing at the man's ignorance. "Not yet, friend," the gambler replied.

Just then they heard gunshots. Four riders came out of the tree line firing at the driver and the man riding shotgun.

"Hang on, folks!" the shotgun yelled.

The driver cracked his whip at the lead horses to get more speed from them. Suddenly the shotgun let out a grunt as a bullet sent him into a nosedive onto the side of the road. Seconds later the driver pulled the coach to a screeching halt. He dropped his whip and raised his hands in surrender.

The outlaws rode up alongside the coach and dismounted. "Everybody out with yer hands up. One funny move and it'll be yer last! Whip, you get down here, too!" The robbers had their hats low and their bandanas high. Only their blazing eyes showed.

The gambler, the pastor and the drifter got out first. The carpetbagger came next and finally the woman. She had a frightened look on her face and appeared confused. The whip stood close by, his hands up high.

The tall, skinny outlaw, the one who had spoken, seemed to be in charge. He had trouble keeping his bandana in place. It kept slipping down over his flattened, broken nose. He suddenly noticed that the gambler and the drifter both wore guns. His eyes narrowed as he stared at them.

"You two, keep yer hands high where we kin see 'em. You try ta grab iron and we'll ventilate the both of ya. Ya git me?"

"Sure," the gambler said sarcastically, "I get you."

The drifter only sneered and spit on the ground. The leader didn't care much for that, so he walked up close and glared into man's eyes.

"I said, did ya git me?"

"Sure, asshole, I get ya."

This rude reply set the leader off like a stick of dynamite. He growled and drove a fist into the drifter's stomach. The drifter grunted and sank to the ground.

"I'll fix you later, fellah," the leader said and backed away. The drifter struggled to his feet and raised his hands again, gasping hard for air. The woman gave him a sympathetic look.

The leader of the outlaws turned to his companions. "Check 'em all out!" he growled, waving the barrel of his gun in the passengers' faces. He stared back at the drifter just to let him know that he would be coming after him as soon as the business of robbing was completed.

"I'll be taking care of you real soon, fellah!" he growled. The drifter smirked in reply but said nothing.

The outlaw chief's three companions moved quickly, roughly searching everyone including the whip. The one big as a grizzly bear, with a potbelly, took the woman's purse and dug into it with huge paws. He took what money was in it and tossed the purse on the ground. The short one went to work robbing the pastor and the carpetbagger while the chubby one cleaned out the gambler, the drifter and the driver.

The three of them held the loot in one hand, staring at it while keeping their guns on the passengers.

"Christ," the big bear complained. "This ain't much, boss. I thought ya said we'd make a killin'.'"

"Take their rings an' watches. Git her earrings!"

They did what they were told, their hands shaking from the cold and wind.

"Whose appaloosa is thet?" the leader asked.

"Mine," the drifter replied. "Why?"

"What's yer name, fellah?"

"Garnett. Jesse Garnett."

"Well, Jesse Garnett, I appreciate you givin' me thet nice horse a yers. Thanks."

Garnett sniffed, lowered one hand and wiped his nose. "How about I draw you for it?"

The outlaw chuckled. "Draw me fer it? What the hell you talkin' about?"

"Me and you. We go for it. You win, you get my horse."

The leader laughed. Garnett smiled.

"It looks like I already got the horse, you fool."

"Afraid?" Garnett asked.

The outlaw's eyes narrowed. The drifter had thrown him a challenge right in front of his men. It was so sudden and unexpected he didn't know how to handle it.

"Hell, boss," the short one said, "drill his ass. We ain't got time ta fart around. It's gittin' too damn cold."

The leader kept staring at Garnett. He didn't like the man's attitude. He should be scared, but he wasn't.

"You think yer hot stuff, do ya, fellah?"

"I'm just saying, let's me and you go for it. Unless you're afraid," Garnett said casually.

The chubby outlaw chuckled. "Heck, boss," he said, "the fool is a-bracin' you! Kin ya beat thet? Haw!"

The outlaw leader pointed the barrel of his gun at Garnett's head. He gritted his teeth. His hand shook with rage. The drifter had put him in a bad position, right in front of his men. The outlaw chief's face was flushed red. The drifter figured he had just gotten himself killed, but suddenly the outlaw smirked and put the gun back in its holster.

"Okay, fellah, you wanna die, then I'll be glade ta oblige ya."

Garnett sighed. That was close. He watched as the outlaw chief backed away about ten feet up the road, away from the coach. A cold wind blew the man's hat off, but he didn't seem to notice. He glared at Garnett with intense hatred. The drifter had put him in a bad position. If he had refused the challenge, he would no longer be able to control his men. He'd lose his status as top dog in the gang, and that would open him up to challenges from his men. To stay on top, you had to be the meanest wolf in the pack.

"Watch this, boys," the outlaw chief growled, "I'm gonna show ya how it's done. Jest like in them Wild West magazines!" He paused a moment to stare at the woman. "Then I'll take thet cute little lady fer a walk in the woods. After I'm finished, you all kin all have a turn wif her." He turned back to Garnett and yelled, "Draw, you yellah-bellied sidewinder!"

The outlaw leader's hand moved fast, but Garnett's hand was a blur as he crouched low and fanned off two shots into the outlaw's heart, knocking him back off the road into the ditch.

The other three were quick to realize what had happened. They dropped their loot and pointed their guns at

Garnett. The gambler saw it, drew with lightning speed and fanned off three shots, dropping the outlaws in a heap on the ground.

Garnett saw what had happened. He nodded "Nice shootin', mister. I owe ya. What's yer handle?"

As they reloaded their guns, the man replied, "Kip Mallory."

"I'm Jesse Garnett." They shook hands.

The coach driver shivered. "Damn, I never saw anything like that before! You two saved us, thet's fer sure!"

Garnett picked his pocket money off the ground. The others did the same. Mallory helped the woman find her stuff. She, the carpetbagger and the pastor got back in the coach while Garnett and Kip Mallory helped the driver put the shotgun's body up on top. They found his rifle down the road where he had been shot.

Garnett stripped the four outlaw bodies of their gunbelts and guns. He and Mallory went through their pockets, collecting what money they had. They put it all in their horses' saddlebags.

"We'll split the horses," Garnett said. "Two each. We can sell them."

"Sure, good idea," Mallory said.

They tied the outlaws' horses to the back of the coach. Mallory got inside the coach while Garnett climbed up beside the driver and got the rifle. Garnett asked, "Where's the next stop?"

"Hood River Station. About ten miles north."

"I'll be riding shotgun. What's your name?"

"Ben. Ben Stewart."

"Let it rip, Ben," Garnett said. "I need a hot cup of coffee."

They pulled into Hood River Station with a howling wind at their backs. The way station had a small beanery, but not much else. They ate while the horses were changed for fresh ones. Garnett and Mallory sat at a table together while the woman sat at a nearby table with the pastor and the carpetbagger.

Garnett noticed the gambler often looked over at the woman. "Pretty, ain't she?" Garnett said.

"Yeah, she sure is. That cute little mouth is driving me crazy."

"I wonder where she's headed?"

"So am I. Maybe I'll get off wherever she does," Mallory said.

Garnett chuckled. "You really got it bad, Mallory. How come? You don't even know her. Or do you?"

The gambler shrugged. "No, but it can hit anybody at any time, Garnett."

Garnett looked sober. "Yeah? Well, I'm still waitin'."

They sat quiet after that. The coach driver, Ben Stewart, came in, got a cup of coffee and sat down with them. "Damn, it's cold out there!" he said.

"How far you gonna carry the shotgun's body?" Garnett asked.

"I'll drop it off at Bremer's Rock."

"How far is that?" Mallory asked.

"Another thirty-five miles," Stewart replied. "But it's a smooth ride so the passengers' kin git a little rest."

"How far will that put us from Ellis?" Garnett asked.

"About a hundred and fifteen miles, give or take a few miles."

"Then we're not even halfway there yet," Mallory said.

"Not until we reach Bremer's Rock. That'll put us halfway."

Mallory nodded. "Where's the woman going?"

"Bremer's Rock."

"The Pastor?"

"Ellis."

"How about the carpetbagger?"

"Ellis, too," Stewart replied. He looked at Garnett. "With that big appaloosa, how come you're riding a stagecoach?"

"It gets cold an' lonesome out there on the trail all alone this time of year. Talking to a horse is a one way conversation. Anyway, I needed a rest and my pal needed a break."

Stewart chuckled. "I get your drift, Garnett."

It was time to leave so they went outside into the cold dark of night. Stewart lit the night lamps clamped to the forward top sides of the stagecoach. They were the kind usually seen on ships at sea.

As the others got back into the stagecoach, Garnett climbed up beside Stewart and pulled his coat collar high. Stewart cracked his whip, and they headed for Bremer's Rock.

Chapter 2

On the way to Bremer's Rock, Kip Mallory cleverly edged the chubby carpetbagger out of his seat next to the woman. The carpetbagger sat next to the pastor on the back bench, looking disappointed. He had envisioned himself and the woman becoming intimate, but the gambler had put a damper on that.

The road was smoother now, and the forward and backward motions of the coach soon had them nodding off. The woman leaned her head against Mallory's shoulder for a moment, then pulled away embarrassed.

"I'm sorry, sir," she said. Her soft voice was pleasing to the gambler's ears.

"Please call me Kip," the gambler said softly.

"Alright, if you want."

What's your name?"

"Michelle. Michelle Logan."

"You're going to Bremer's Rock, are you?"

"Yes."

"First trip?"

"Yes."

She shivered and Mallory took his jacket off and put it around her shoulders, atop her light coat. She looked up into his eyes for a moment and said, "Thank you." Mallory stared at the small, pretty woman. She looked to be about his own age, thirty. From the sound of her voice he figured she was from the East. "Where are you from?" he asked

"East of here, Pittsburgh," she said almost as if she were proud of it and a bit regretful for leaving.

He wanted to ask her if she had a man, but decided not to be that bold. If she did, it didn't matter. A woman could always change her mind. Maybe she was involved with the wrong man. That was always possible. For some reason, it felt good just to be next to her. It was as if they had known each other for a long time, perhaps in another life.

Mallory spoke her name softly. "Michelle. It's a beautiful name."

"Thank you," she said, blushing.

18

"Don't be offended, but I think you're beautiful."

She looked across at the carpetbagger and the pastor to see if they were listening. They appeared to be dozing. "That's nice, but you shouldn't talk like that."

"Why not?"

"Because we don't know each other."

"No, but we can take care of that, real fast."

She said nothing, and they sat quietly in the darkness of the coach. The oil lamps bolted to the topside sputtered and cast dancing shadows on the road.

When they pulled into the town of Bremer's Rock, it was around two in the morning. The stage stop was at the edge of town, alongside the coach road. It was an impressive two story frame building with torches on high poles blazing out front. A big sign read:

Welcome to Bremer's Rock

Courtesy of the Branford & Smith Coach Line

Stewart announced a forty-five minute layover. He got the woman's suitcase from the rear boot and set it on the porch. She was the only one not going on ahead to Ellis.

The station was a full service station with a café and bar. There were rooms on the second floor where travelers could rest or stay overnight.

Bremer's Rock also had a telegraph setup. Stewart used it to send a wire to his headquarters in Ellis informing them of the holdup and the death of the shotgun. Attendants came from the rear of the station and removed the body.

"What will they do with it?" Garnett asked.

"They'll take it up to Ellis by buckboard."

"Did you know him well?" Mallory asked.

"Yeah. I know his family, too," Stewart replied. "He was a good kid. I'm glad you and Mallory shot those bastards."

They all went inside except Mallory and Michelle Logan, who stood together on the porch. He stared at her while she looked down, fidgeting nervously with her gloves.

"Won't you come inside for a cup of coffee, Michelle?"

"I shouldn't. Someone is coming to pick me up."

"You'll freeze out here. They can find you inside."

She was undecided for a moment, then nodded. "Alright, I will."

As they went inside, she realized she still had his coat over her shoulders. She removed it and handed it to him. They went into the café and sat at a table away from the others. There was a large fireplace blazing at one end of the room. A table was set up with a large urn of coffee and a selection of fruit tarts and crullers, courtesy of the stage line. They took what they wanted and sat down to eat. When they were finished, they sat and made idle talk for a while. It was as if they were old friends.

Mallory said, "I wish you didn't have to go."

"It's been arranged."

"What's been arranged?"

She was about to answer when a man who worked for the stage line came into the café and walked over to their table.

"Are you Miss Logan, ma'am?"

"Yes, I am."

"There's a man outside with a buckboard. He says he was sent to pick you up."

"Thank you. Please tell him I'll be right there."

After the man left, Michelle stood up and offered Mallory her hand.

"I guess this is goodbye, Kip," she said.

"I'll walk outside with you."

He walked alongside her as they went outside onto the porch. A cowboy was loading Michelle's suitcase into a buckboard. Michelle hesitated for a moment and then glanced up into Mallory's eyes before she let the cowboy help her up on the bench. For a moment, he thought he read something in that glance, almost a plea to intervene, to stop her from going on. The gambler watched as the buckboard went down the road and around a bend out of sight. As Mallory walked back into the café he saw the stage lineman, the one who had come looking for Michelle.

"Say, pal, whose buckboard was that?"

"It belongs to the Circle H Ranch," he answered as if the Circle H was something special.

"What's the Circle H? Never heard of it."

"That because you ain't from around here. It's the biggest ranch in the area. Six hundred thousand acres and more. It's owned by Harlan Preston."

"What's her connection with it?" Mallory asked hesitantly, almost afraid to hear the answer.

"I thought you knew her, since she was with you inside."

"No, I only met her on the stagecoach coming up from Sterling."

"Well, I never saw her before, either."

"Is this Preston married?"

"Not now. His wife died a while back. He's been a widower ever since."

Mallory pondered that for a moment, then asked, "How's the gambling situation around here?"

"Not too bad, being as there's a lot of ranches and cowboys around. What's yer game?"

"Cards, mostly poker," Mallory said.

"Then yer in the right place, friend. Bremer's Rock has lots a gamblin'."

Mallory went inside. He found Garnett and Stewart at a table in the bar. "I'll need my bags," he said to Stewart.

"You staying?"

"Yeah. I heard this is a good town for gamblers." Garnett smiled. He knew it was the girl, not the gambling. "How about you, Garnett? Wanna stick around a few days?"

"I promised Stewart here I'd ride shotgun up to Ellis."

Mallory gave this some thought and said, "Then you can come back on the return stage. Leave your horse at the stable. Pick it up when you get back here."

Garnett looked over at Stewart. "Could I do that?"

"Sure. I'll be in Ellis for a day, before heading back to the train depot in Sterling again. I'll be stopping here as I swing south."

"Hell," Garnett said to Mallory, "Sure. I got no place special to be."

Aside from that, he liked Kip Mallory. They were two different peas in the same pod. Anyway, he owed Mallory his life for covering his back with those outlaws.

It was agreed that Garnett would leave his appaloosa at the town stable. Mallory would arrange to sell the four outlaw horses, the saddles and tack. When Garnett got back from Ellis, they would split the money down the middle.

They shook on it and Garnett got up alongside Stewart and rode shotgun all the way to Ellis, eighty miles northwest.

Chapter 3

The name Bremer's Rock referred to a huge rock where a man named Eli Bremer struck gold in 1849. There was no gold in the rock, but there was plenty of gold in the hills behind it. The rock became the landmark for people who came looking for the place where Bremer had struck it rich.

People of all kinds came to Bremer's Rock, but the law never did. The only law was the law of the gun and knife in that remote section of the wide open Kansas plains. When the gold ran out in the 1860s, the prospectors left in a hurry. A few years later, the ranchers and the cattle came in to support what little of the town that was still there.

There wasn't much in the way of law enforcement. Ranchers settled their differences as they saw fit. It all boiled down to who had the most fire power, and who had the meanest cowboys backing them up. That eventually turned out to be Harlan Preston and his Circle H cowboys. Everyone in the Bremer's Rock area feared them.

Harlan Preston had come up from dry, sandy south Texas with a small herd of a thousand cattle and settled in the lush, green valley of Bremer's Rock. It was all open, free land. Preston staked out a chunk big enough for three hundred thousand head of cattle because he intended to grow his herd to that size.

The location of the Circle H was ideal. Ellis was eighty miles to the northwest and Sterling was eighty miles to the south. As cattle drives go, it was a five day drive to either cattle town, following the coach road. Since the stage line had built a full service stage stop with a telegraph office at Bremer's Rock that was to Preston's advantage, too. Everything worked out just fine for him.

In the early days, after coming to Bremer's Rock, Preston met and married a woman whom he worshipped for her beauty and goodness. He gave her all his love and she returned it tenfold. They were happy for many years. When she became with child, Preston was overjoyed by the good news. Then his life took a sad turn when she had a complicated delivery, and both she and the child died. After she passed away, something died inside Preston. He lost the ability to love another woman.

Nevertheless, at the age of forty-five, Preston decided he had mourned long enough and went looking for a companion. Not a wife, just a companion, someone to fill his empty home. He found her in a twenty-five-year old dance hall beauty in Ellis. She became his mistress and went to live at the Circle H Ranch. Smart in business, Preston was naive when it came to women. She saw very little of him as he ran his empire.

His constant neglect of his mistress had dire consequences. An informant told him that she was being indiscreet. One day he followed the girl to a deserted line shack where she and her cowboy lover had been meeting on a regular basis. The cowboy, who worked for the Box N brand, was young, handsome and reckless.

In a fit of rage, Preston shot them both and burned down the line shack with their bodies in it. No one had seen what he had done except God and the devil. Rumors grew and circulated around as to who had done it, but no one had the nerve to say Preston's name outright.

For years after that, Preston was a lonely, bitter man. He was also much feared for the way he treated people. He made it clear that any cattle straying onto his land would be his to rebrand. Any cowboys from other ranches found on his land would be hanged as trespassers. Strangers who accidently crossed onto Circle H land would suffer the same fate. Preston was a law unto himself.

One day, while at a cattlemen's convention in Sterling, he took time to do some shopping for hats and boots. He saw a young woman clerk in a department store who caught his attention. She was very pretty. He asked her out to dinner. At first she refused, but after he asked four days in a row she finally gave in.

Her name was Michelle Logan. She was a shy woman, thirty years old. Originally from Pittsburgh, she heard that the West was a good place for jobs, so she took a train to Kansas City. After living there for a while, she worked her way further west to Sterling, with a girlfriend. They separated when the girlfriend married and moved to Texas.

Preston took her to a fine restaurant. She was impressed with his good manners and the way he treated her, even though he was much older than she was. She had dated clerks at the department store, but they never took her to upscale restaurants to eat fancy food and drink champagne.

As for Preston, he was thinking of his future and the future of his empire, and this beautiful woman fitted right in. One day, over dinner, he put a proposal to her. He asked her to be the mother of his child.

"What if it's a girl?" she asked.

"No matter, boy or girl."

"What do I get?"

"Ten thousand dollars. I'll put five in a bank account when you're with child and give you the rest when you deliver."

It sounded cold and businesslike, but ten thousand dollars was an awful lot of money. "You're very blunt," Michelle said. "What if I say no?"

Preston shrugged. "I'll ask someone else, then."

Michelle knew there were at least ten young girls that worked in her store who would jump at the offer of ten thousand dollars. After all, it was years and years of wages. Just the thought of having that much money overwhelmed her common sense.

"It's just a business arrangement, isn't it?" she asked.

"Of course, nothing more."

"Can I think about it?"

"I'll give you until tomorrow night at dinner. After that I'll ask someone else." Preston knew how to keep the pressure on.

Michelle Logan went home to her dark, little cold-water flat and thought about her situation. She was poor and would always be poor. But having a child and giving it away would be hard to do. Yet, on the other hand, the child would become wealthy and someday inherit a huge ranch. And there was always the possibility that she could, one day, reveal herself as the mother. So perhaps this was a chance for her to become financially secure.

The next night at dinner, she told Harlan Preston she would accept his offer. She expected him to be happy and excited, but he was unemotional and businesslike.

"Good," he said. "A wise decision, Michelle."

Before he left, he gave her traveling money and stagecoach fare to Bremer's Rock. She had never traveled any long distances by stage before. Bremer's Rock was eighty miles from Sterling, a six or seven hour ride by stagecoach. She was to leave on the noon stage on Monday.

On Monday morning, Michelle was at the stage depot waiting for the stagecoach. It didn't arrive until two in the afternoon due to a broken wheel. It was further delayed for a change of horses. She finally got on with several other passengers, a pastor, a carpetbagger, a drifter and a handsome looking man who kept staring at her.

By the time they reached Bremer's Rock a lifetime had passed before her eyes. A handsome young man named Kip Mallory had befriended her, comforted her, and saved her from outlaws. It was as if fate had arranged for them to meet. All he had to do was stop her from getting in that buckboard. She was his to have. He must have seen that in her eyes, the way she looked at him. But he never stopped her.

That fateful night, as the buckboard took her away from Bremer's Rock, Mallory stood looking on. She knew he was watching her until the buckboard turned a bend in the road. He disappeared from her life. She would never see him again.

"How far is it?" she asked the cowboy, after a long time on the winding road to the Circle H Ranch.

"About an hour more, ma'am."

At that moment, it all suddenly came rushing upon her. She fully realized, for the first time, just what the bargain with this man really meant. Now that she was here, she knew it was all a mistake. She could never go through with it. If she had never met Kip Mallory, she might not have had any regrets. Now, all too late, she realized she was in love with him.

Back in Sterling it had seemed so romantic, a rich cattle baron wanting her to give him an heir. It was like a romance novel where, in the end, the cattle baron fell in love with the woman and married her. But this was not that story. Suddenly, Michelle felt like a lamb going to the slaughter. She had to somehow, get herself out of this mess. Perhaps it was best to tell him how she felt about Mallory. He might understand, let her out of the bargain and send her on her way.

All these thoughts raced through Michelle Logan's mind as she sat shivering on the bench of the buckboard. The ride seemed to end all too fast. She suddenly found herself in a large, two story ranch house standing in front of Harlan Preston. They exchanged greetings. He saw how nervous she acted.

"Are you alright, Michelle?" he asked. She seemed distant.

"I'm very tired, Harlan. The trip on the stagecoach was pretty uncomfortable."

"Of course. Maria will show you to your room and you can refresh yourself. I'll see you for dinner."

He called out and an old woman came from the kitchen to show her up to her room. It turned out she was his cook but did other chores around the house, too. She was also a midwife.

"I will deliver the baby when it comes," Maria said flatly, without emotion.

"How nice," was all Michelle could think of saying.

For some reason she was embarrassed and wondered if Preston had told the old lady the conditions of their relationship, that she was being paid to give away her child. It made her feel like someone hired to do a particular task, and, after the task was done, she was no longer of any use. At dinner that night, Michelle asked him for time to adjust.

"Of course, take all the time you need," Preston told her.

As the days passed by, she began to learn that he was not a romantic man. A little compassion on his part would have helped put her at ease, but Harlan Preston was totally absorbed in running his cattle empire. He rose before sunrise, and she didn't see him until evening.

She caught parts of conversations about what went on at the Circle H Ranch, about his conflict with the other cattlemen. Once she even heard something about hanging a trespasser. A week later there was talk about shooting a cowboy and dragging the body over to the other ranch. He was caught taking back his own cattle that had drifted onto Preston's property.

Sometimes Preston was gone for two or three days at a stretch. When he came back to the ranch, he spent most of his time in his study doing paperwork. If he wasn't there, he was down in the bunkhouse talking to his men.

After putting him off for three weeks Michelle finally decided to tell him flat out that she couldn't go through with the plan. The truth was, now that she had seen the other side of him, she was afraid. Would he do the same thing to her that he did to those unfortunate cowboys who strayed onto his precious land? It frightened her just to think about it. She didn't know what to do. She felt trapped.

One night he approached her and said, "I think we should get it done this weekend." The mechanical way he said it turned her cold.

"I need more time, Harlan. I'm sorry."

"It's been several weeks, that's long enough."

"But, you said I could take all the time I needed."

"I've changed my mind," he said. "I want it done and over with."

"What's the rush?"

"I want you with child as soon as possible. After that I won't bother you because you'll be carrying." He paused for a moment. "I'm not getting any younger and neither are you."

"Please give me more time."

He sighed. "Alright. I'm going away on business for a week. When I come back, you'll hold up your end of the bargain." Those words left her frightened. It sounded like he would take her against her will.

After Preston left on his business trip, Michelle broke down and cried. It all suddenly seemed like a horrible nightmare from which she couldn't awake. She cursed herself for being such a fool. She decided to bolt, to run.

Packing her suitcase, she went outside to get someone to take her to Bremer's Rock. Everyone ignored her. They wouldn't even look at her. Each one she approached walked away. She soon realized that she was a prisoner.

Word of Michelle's situation soon got out when a Circle H cowboy let it slip during idol talk in a bar in Bremer's Rock. Her name soon cropped up during every poker game in every saloon in town. One of the poker players just happened to be Kip Mallory. He was sitting in on his last poker game before heading for Ellis when a cowboy from the Circle H started talking.

"Yeah," Carl, the cowboy, said, "Ol' Preston has got himself in a fix, alright."

"What's thet?" one of the players from town named Sid asked.

"He's got this pretty thing out at the ranch who's supposed ta sire his colt. But the rumor is, she don't wanna go through with the deal. It's only a matter of time before ol' Preston lays down the law."

"What the heck is he gonna do, take her by force?" someone asked.

"Knowin' how Preston operates, that's exactly what he'll do," Carl replied.

"What's her name, do you know?" Mallory asked out of curiosity.

"She's got a fancy name. Starts with an M."

"Michelle?" Kip Mallory asked.

"Yeah, why? Do you know her?" Carl asked.

"She came up on the same stage as me from Sterling a few weeks ago. No, I don't know her," Mallory replied. Later that night while lying in his bed at the hotel, Kip Mallory made a decision.

He was going to go out to the Circle H and rescue Michelle Logan.

Chapter 4

After saying goodbye to Kip Mallory at Bremer's Rock, Jesse Garnett took up his position next to Ben Stewart on the bench of the stagecoach. He reached under and got the rifle as Stewart cracked the whip to get the four horses moving. It was four in the morning and the next stop was West Fork, ten miles northwest. Inside the coach, bundled up against the cold and wind, were the pastor and the carpetbagger.

"How long you been whip?" Garnett hollered above the rattling of the coach wheels on the hard road.

"Two years now," Stewart replied. "This is strictly a passenger coach. I don't pick up any mail. Another coach does that. It picks up and delivers mail and cargo from Sterling to Ellis and all the towns in between and back. It's heavily guarded because of the robberies."

"Sounds like big business," Garnett said. "Passengers, mail and cargo. Seven days a week?"

"Yeah, but we ain't that big. We're just a connecting line between Ellis and Sterling. People who want to travel further west, say to California, will go to Ellis to catch the Union Pacific. If they're going south, they catch the Atchison Topeka and Santa Fe from Sterling."

Garnett nodded. The shouting was too hard on the voice so he didn't ask any more questions.

An hour later, at the crack of dawn, they rolled into West Fork, ten miles north of Bremer's Rock. They picked up a family of three, a husband, wife and little boy. With the pastor and the carpetbagger, that made five in all.

The next stop was Kingston's Corners, another ten miles further north. They changed horses again, had a half-hour layover and took on two more passengers, both carpetbaggers.

After Kingston's Corners, they suffered along twenty-five miles of curving, bumpy, hilly road. It was eleven in the morning when they arrived dusty, deaf and exhausted in Jubilee Flats. The town was bustling with activity.

"Jubilee Flats, folks!" Stewart announced. "Rest rooms and food are available. We'll be leavin' in about forty-five minutes."

They changed horses again in Jubilee Flats and started out for Ellis a little after noontime with two new passengers, a young man and a woman.

"How far is Ellis?" Garnett asked.

"Another thirty-five miles. And it ain't gonna be pretty, so hang on to yer hat!"

The last thirty-five mile stretch was a treacherous trek over a winding road leading up steep hills and down long slopes that left the coach brakes smoking red hot from friction.

Ten miles from Ellis the hills gave way to a long, flat plain. Here, vicious winds rocked the coach from side-to-side as if it were a toy. Clouds of thick, suffocating dust filtered inside making everyone inside cough and choke. Eyes burned and tears ran down cheeks as the passengers held whatever they could find over their faces.

Tumbleweed flew across the flat ground, piling up against the coach, collecting under its belly and getting caught in the spokes where it was stuck fast. Inside they could feel the vibration and hear the cracking of the dry brush as the wheels ground it into tiny pieces. Three miles away, Ellis poked its head above the horizon like an oasis in the desert.

Stewart guided the coach into the main station of the Branford & Smith Light Coach Transfer Line in the middle of town. The passengers got off with sore backs and clothing covered with a fine, sandy silt. Attendants came out, unloaded the baggage, and drove the coach around back to the maintenance building and corral. After picking up their belongings, the passengers headed in different directions. The carpetbagger went into the station café for a hot meal, the pastor walked off someplace, and the family of three and the couple headed for the train depot.

"Follow me," Ben Stewart told Garnett.

Garnett followed him into the office, a wing attached to the left side of the station. A man came from behind a desk to greet the driver.

"You alright, Ben?"

"Yes, Mr. Branford. Did Jim's body get here okay?"

"Yes, as a matter of fact it came in last night."

Stewart nodded at Garnett. "This is Jesse Garnett, sir. He and another fellah got the drop on the robbers. Sent all four of them to hell. He rode shotgun with me all the way from Bremer's Rock."

Branford, a short, pudgy businessman with a bald head, had a cigar in his mouth. He removed it and offered Garnett his hand. "Mr. Garnett, we owe you a debt of gratitude. Thank you, sir, for your service." He turned to a nearby table where a female clerk was busy making entries in a ledger. "Myra, get Mr. Garnett two hundred dollars from petty cash. Bill it to overhead."

"It's not necessary, sir," Garnett said.

"Nonsense, Mr. Garnett, you earned every cent of it."

The amount impressed Garnett. He said nothing more and, when the clerk handed him four fifty-dollar bank bills, he folded them and put them in his shirt pocket.

"How would you like to ride shotgun for the Branford & Smith Line, Garnett?" Mr. Branford asked.

The request came suddenly, throwing Garnett off balance for a moment. As he considered it, the pain in his back got his attention. Sitting up on that hard bench while the coach bucked like a wild stallion was not what he would want to do the rest of his life. Considering that and the possibility of being shot, Garnett declined the offer.

"Right now, sir, I have a commitment back in Bremer's Rock. Maybe I'll take you up on your offer when I'm finished there."

"Good enough," Branford said. "It's an open offer, Garnett, so keep that in mind, won't you?"

"I surely will, sir."

Stewart and Garnett left. Once out in front of the station, they stopped to talk.

"I'm single like you, Garnett. So, how about we do some socializing? There's three saloons in town needin' our attention."

Garnett chuckled. "Heck, why not? But I need to shake the dust off my rags and take a bath first."

"Come on, I'll take you over to the barbershop. There's some of those fancy metal bathtubs over there. They got a Chinese girl who washes and dries yer clothes, too. All for six bits."

"Sounds good."

Garnett followed Ben Stewart down the busy street to a huge canvas tent two blocks from the station. They stopped at the entrance, paid a Chinese man six bits each and stepped inside onto a plank corridor. The corridor ran down the length of the tent past partitioned off cubicles.

In each cubicle was a large, oval, galvanized tub that sat off the ground on wooden blocks. There was also a chair and a small, square table with a box of lye soap bars on it. Along with the soap was a brush and a tiny mirror. A small wool rug lay on the planks in front of the tub.

On the way in, Garnett noticed about a dozen Chinese men in the backyard working over huge cauldrons of steaming water that hung above large fire pits. The men wore sandals and were stripped down to their waists. Their muscular bodies glistened, despite the chill in the air.

Two of these men came and quickly filled the tubs halfway up with hot water, then left. Garnett undressed. He dropped his worn wool suit and other clothing on the chair, put his gunbelt on the table and then eased his body slowly into the hot water. Moments later a Chinese girl came with a large, freshly washed brown cotton bath towel. She put it over the back of the chair.

"You want me to wash you?" she asked, in passable English.

"Ah, no, ma'am," Garnett said quickly. She emptied his pockets, took his hat, suit and other clothing and left.

The two men couldn't see one another because of the canvas walls, but they were close enough to carry on a conversation.

"Ain't this great?" Stewart asked. "We've got the whole place to ourselves."

"Sure is. I could go to sleep and never wake up," Garnett chuckled.

"Yeah, me too."

Garnett reached over to the table, grabbed a bar of soap and the brush and then went to work scrubbing his body parts. Steam from the hot water flowed up in the air. Outside, the wind blew against the tent. Garnett felt as if he was in a safe, warm cocoon. After he had scrubbed himself good, he settled back in the water.

"Yeah," Stewart called over to him. "We'll have a good time. It's on me, pal."

"Sounds like fun," Garnett answered.

"I feel like a nap," Stewart said with a chuckle. "I think I'll take ten."

"Sounds like a plan," Garnett replied.

Garnett reached over to the table and got the makings. Soon, he was lying back in the water smoking. When he was finished, he dropped the butt over the side of the tub, lay back in the water and closed his eyes.

He was about to doze off when he heard footsteps and strange voices coming from Stewart's cubicle. They didn't sound friendly. One voice said, "Keep quiet or I'll drill ya! An' git them hands up where I can see 'em!"

"Sure," Stewart replied. "The money is over there, on the chair."

"Git his gun first!" a different voice said urgently.

"Don't worry, I got it," the first voice replied.

Garnett quickly reached over, pulled his Colt from its holster and lowered it into the water. He lay back pretending to be asleep. Seconds later a man carrying a double-barreled shotgun walked into his cubicle.

"Wake up, fool!" the shotgun man said.

Garnett pretended to wake up. He rubbed his eyes with his left hand while watching the outlaw. The man kept the shotgun pointed at him as he grabbed up the two hundred dollars in bank bills. He stared at them as if he'd struck gold.

"Shit!" the outlaw said, staring at the money. "Looks like about two hundred bucks ta me!" He turned and yelled over to his companion. "We done struck it rich, pal!"

"Great!" the other man called back from Stewart's side.

As the shotgun man stuffed the money in his pants, Garnett brought his Colt up out of the water. The shotgun man heard the noise and looked towards Garnett. Garnett shot him in the chest, knocking him to the ground. As he fell dying, the intruder fired off a wild shot that blew a hole in the bottom of the bathtub. There was an eerie silence as the water gushed out of the tub onto the ground.

Suddenly the outlaw in Stewart's cubicle called out. "What happened, Ed?" Ed didn't answer and neither did Garnett. He waited with his gun up.

Suddenly the other outlaw peeked around the corner of the cubicle, looking to see what had happened. When he saw his friend lying on the ground he rushed at Garnett, firing the gun he had taken from Stewart. His shot went wild, narrowly missing Garnett's head. Garnett shot him in the heart and he collapsed on top of his partner.

After a short silence, Garnett yelled, "You okay, Stewart?"

"Yeah! You?"

"Yeah. I got them both."

Stewart laughed nervously. "Jesus. I thought they killed you, Garnett."

People came running into the tent from every direction. Before he knew it, there were townspeople and Chinese everywhere he looked. Stewart came in with a towel around his waist. He saw the big hole in the end of Garnett's bathtub where the water was still running out. "Damn, you almost got a free foot massage."

"Yeah."

The owner came in with a deputy marshal. Garnett hunkered down in the tub to keep from exposing his lower body parts. The deputy glanced down at the bodies and laughed. Ben Stewart looked at the deputy and asked, "What's so funny, Tom?"

"Them two, Ben. I was wonderin' when their luck was gonna run out. They finally bought the farm. Who did it?"

"My partner here. They robbed me and then went for him. He was ready for 'em."

"Quite a town you have here, Deputy," Garnett said. "A fellow can't even take a bath without getting his jewels shot off."

The deputy laughed again. "It looks ta me like it was these two who got the sticky end of the stick."

The owner began to apologize, offering Stewart and Garnett free baths for a month. He even offered them their money back. Garnett grabbed a towel, wrapped it around his waist and stepped out of the tub. He separated the two bodies and got his two hundred dollars from the shirt of the man called Ed. After that, the deputy had the dead bodies dragged away. The owner shooed away the onlookers.

When they finally left, Stewart said, "Damn, Garnett, that was close! I need a drink to steady my nerves. How about you, pal?"

Garnett nodded. "Yeah, an' maybe more than just one, partner."

They waited half an hour for their clothing. The girl brought them back cleaned, ironed and smelling fresh. Garnett and Stewart dressed and left.

Stewart knew the town well. He took Garnett to a bar three blocks away from the bathhouse. It was a huge place called the European Emporium. Gamblers and businessmen rubbed elbows at the bar and poker tables. It was fairly upscale, fancier than any other saloon that Garnett had ever been in. The prices at the bar were steep.

"I'm buying, Garnett," Stewart said. "Put your money away, friend." The whiskey was as upscale as the place and went down smooth as silk. "Good red eye, ain't it?" Stewart said.

"Better than good, Ben. Darn good. Let's tie one on!" Garnett yelled against the background noise. He felt happy to be alive.

"Sure, why the heck not?" Stewart replied.

Six rounds later things began to happen. Garnett and Stewart got into a fight with some customers and were thrown out onto the street. They staggered across town to another bar, got in a fight there also and ended out on the street again. The two just couldn't seem to behave themselves.

Finally, they got their butts kicked by four cowboys and ended up in an alley sitting on their backsides.

"I know another place where they're jest gonna love us," Stewart said. "It's much nicer."

Garnett chuckled. "Where's that? Dodge City?"

"Nope, down by the stockyards. It might smell a little like cows, but the company is better."

"Okay," Garnett said. "Let's give it a try." They both had trouble standing up, but finally got to their feet. "Are you drunk, Ben?" Garnett asked

"Nope. Are you, Jesse?"

Garnett lied. "Shucks, no."

"Good, then let's go to Candy's Place."

"Who's Candy?"

"C'mon. You'll see."

They made their way down to the south side of town where the railroad tracks ran east and west. A large building there had once been a warehouse but was now a dance hall.

Dozens of horses and buckboards were tied up in front and in a nearby field. Cowboys and townsfolk walked towards it in a steady stream.

A sign over the twin doors read, "Candy's Dance Hall." Overhead oil lamps softly lighted the inside, and soft music flowed out through the windows and doors.

They paid two bits to enter and hung their gunbelts on a numbered peg on the wall near the doors. Once inside, they bought ten dance tickets at a booth.

"The gals are over there," Stewart said, pointing.

As they walked from the booth down a hallway to the dance hall their heads cleared up a little, but Garnett still felt somewhat foggy. He stared around and saw they were in a big open area with a sawdust covered dance floor.

On one side of the place was an area resembling a corral where three dozen or so girls of differing ages sat on chairs. It was a busy area. A bunch of cowboys and men in suits were gathered there choosing dance partners. Girls of all shapes and sizes stepped through a gate as the men selected them by handing them a ticket.

"What's that all about?" Garnett asked, trying to focus his eyes and act sober.

"The girls cash the tickets in when the place closes up about two in the morning. They get a penny a dance."

"Whatta we do?" Garnett asked.

"Pick a gal you like and give her a ticket every time you dance with her. It's easy. Ya kin change girls, if you want to."

Garnett shrugged. His brain was only half awake. "Sure," he heard himself saying.

Ben Stewart pointed at a girl in a dark brown dress. She walked up to him. He tore a ticket from his strip and offered it to her. Stewart grabbed her hand and they went off to dance. A band played slow music somewhere in a far corner. The dance floor was mostly in shadows and Stewart and the girl quickly disappeared out of sight.

Garnett stood unsteady on his feet staring at the strip of dance tickets in his hand. He was undecided as to whether he wanted to dance or not, thinking that in his condition he'd probably step on someone's toes. The girls noticed his indecision. "I wonder what farm he's from?" one of them remarked. This brought laughter from her companions. Several of the girls walked up to the rail and waved for him to come over. He was about to go see what they wanted when someone came up behind him and put a hand on his arm.

Garnett turned and saw a woman. She stood very close, staring up at him. Her eyes searched his face as if he were someone she had known in times past and never expected to see again, like he was someone close to her who had died and suddenly come back to life. He smiled down at her as her gaze traveled back and forth over his face. Finally, their eyes met and locked.

"Hi…" was all Garnett could manage to say.

The woman was pleasingly pretty with hair the color of autumn leaves and large, green eyes like a mountain cat. She had those large freckles high on her cheeks that most red headed women have, giving her a youthful look. Her dress was blue and frilly but conservative, a full length affair that covered her neck and arms. The only thing exposed was her face and hair. But that was enough to hold Garnett's attention.

"You look so much like him," she said softly.

Without another word, she took his hand, led him over to the dance floor, then put her left arm up over his right shoulder. Her soft, warm fingers came to rest on the back of his neck as she took his left arm and placed it around her waist. She fitted very comfortably into his arms.

"My name is Candy Clarkson," she said softly. "What's yours?"

"I just forgot," Garnett replied.

"You remind me of someone I loved."

Garnett fought the fog in his head, trying to say something intelligent, something with meaning. "My name is Jesse Garnett and I just took a bath, ma'am," was the best he could come up with.

Candy Clarkson smiled and said, "Good for you, Jesse Garnett."

Garnett chuckled. "Did I just die and go to heaven?"

"Not yet."

She put her head against Garnett's right shoulder. He could feel her breath warm against his neck. She smelled like a thousand roses.

"You're killing me, ma'am," he said.

"That'll come later," she whispered in his ear.

She guided Garnett around the floor to the rhythm of a waltz. He began to sober up very quickly.

Chapter 5

Kip Mallory sat in his room above the way station thinking about Michelle Logan. The knowledge that rancher Harlan Preston was holding her against her will pained him deeply. He remembered that uncertain, pleading look on her face as she climbed into the buckboard and was driven away to Preston's ranch. It was as if she had been begging him to rescue her and take her away with him to a safe place. But he had failed her. He had stood helpless, not raising a hand to help her as the buckboard drove her to an uncertain fate. Mallory silently cursed himself for being weak.

He had never felt so connected to a woman before. She was the one. He knew it and he felt she knew it. He had seen it in her lovely blue eyes. Now she was being held against her will, and there was no one she could turn to. She was caught in a trap of her own making and couldn't escape it. Michelle desperately needed his help and Kip knew he had to save her.

His plan was to get her to Ellis where they would take a train west to California. On the other hand, if she wanted to, she could walk away and he would know it was all just a momentary fancy, an illusion. In any case, she would at least be free of this evil man, Preston.

Last week, Mallory sold one of his two outlaw horses but kept the other one for Michelle. Now he knew he had to act or it would be too late. He had the directions. All he had to do was to take the road that led west from Bremer's Rock. After ten miles, the road came to a fork that ran east and west. West led to the Circle H Ranch.

All that day, Mallory was excited waiting for the right time to leave. About three hours before dark he got the horses together and set out on his journey. It was a crisp, cool day with heavy clouds above. He reached the perimeter of the ranch before sundown, but kept riding until he came to a hill overlooking the ranch house yard.

After tying the horses to a scrub oak, he crept forward until he had a good view of everything below. He could see the cowboys of the Circle H walking about doing chores, and playing horseshoes. Some stood around talking and smoking. Dogs barked, chickens cackled and pigs squealed. Time seemed to stand still until finally dusk set in. Mallory moved swiftly.

Running in a crouch, he snuck up to the back side of the ranch house, away from the yard, and looked into the kitchen window. He saw an old woman sitting at a table, smoking and reading a magazine by the light of an oil lamp. Mallory walked slowly past the kitchen to the south side of the house. Looking in the window, he saw Michelle in the living room reading a magazine.

Suddenly he heard footsteps and he dropped flat on the ground. A dark figure walked within five feet of him. It moved across the yard in the direction of the bunkhouse. When he stood up and looked back into the window, Michelle was gone. He wondered if she had gone upstairs to bed. If so, all was lost. He could never get to her unless he went directly into the house, and that was out of the question.

Suddenly he heard a voice from the front of the house. "Good evenin', ma'am."

Mallory slowly crept around to the front of the house to the side of the porch, keeping low again. He saw a cowboy salute Michelle as she stood on the porch in the shadows. He waited until the cowboy walked down to the corral, then walked slowly around to the porch steps. The darkness hid his identity as he stood by the steps looking up at her. "Michelle!" he whispered.

For a moment she didn't react, then she quietly gasped in surprise. "Kip? Is that you?"

"Yes."

"What are you doing here?"

"I came to get you."

"You can't. It's too dangerous. They'll kill you."

"I have two horses waiting."

"I can't ride. I don't know how."

Mallory paused to look around. "It's alright. I'll show you how."

She glanced backward into the house for a moment. "Alright, but I have to get my coat and purse."

"Please hurry!"

Michelle turned and went into the house. Mallory waited at the bottom of the porch steps. The wind blew across the yard, gathering dust. A dog came running up from the barn.

When it saw Mallory, it stopped to stare at him, then began to bark and growl.

As Mallory backed away, it rushed him. He lashed out with a boot and sent it tumbling on the ground. It quickly got up and rushed him a second time.

"In here!" Michelle quickly opened the door and Mallory ran into the hallway next to her. They heard voices in the yard. The dog barked and charged the door.

"Something is going on," someone shouted out front. Boots pounded up the porch steps.

"Follow me!" Michelle whispered as she struggled into her coat while holding her purse. As they ran into the kitchen, the old woman dropped her magazine and looked up in surprise. "I'm leaving," Michelle said. The old woman shrugged as they ran out onto the kitchen porch.

Once outside, Mallory said, "Up there!" He pointed to the hill and they ran across the lawn and up the rise. At the top, they stood panting for air.

"I don't know what to do," Michelle said.

Mallory grabbed her in his arms and swung her up into the saddle. He put her hands on the saddle horn. "Just hang on to it!" he said as he adjusted the stirrups. "Put your feet in here!"

He mounted up, grabbed the reins of her horse and got them moving into the woods. It was now dark and he suddenly realized that he hadn't planned the whole thing very well. He had no idea which way to go. To make things worse, he heard the baying of bloodhounds down in the ranch yard.

Preston's men were getting ready to come after them.

Chapter 6

Ben Stewart had delayed leaving the Ellis station for twenty minutes, hoping Jesse Garnett would show up as he said he would. The young man sitting beside him in the box shifted nervously, anxious to get on the road. Stewart gave out a big sigh and was about to crack his whip when Garnett came running up the street.

"Sorry, old pal!" Garnett said, staring up at Stewart and the young man beside him on the bench.

"This is Tobey Richards, the new shotgun," Stewart said.

"Howdy, Richards!" Garnett replied.

"Jump in," Stewart told Garnett. "We're runnin' late."

Garnett nodded, pulled the coach door open and got in just as Ben Stewart cracked the whip. He lurched back into his seat, pulling the door closed behind him. The stagecoach gave a jerk and moved out. A horse, tied to the boot ramp, was startled. It whinnied and trotted along behind the coach.

Once seated, Garnett nodded to the six passengers and settled into a corner by a window. Pulling his hat low and his coat collar high, he let his chin drop in an effort to take a nap.

Instead of falling asleep, he thought about Candy Clarkson. He could still smell her perfume and feel the touch of her lips. She told him her husband had died two years ago, and when she saw Garnett walk into the dance hall she thought she was seeing his ghost. She asked him if he was interested into going into business with her, opening another dance hall in Hays City or Russell. He told her about his plans to open a mercantile, hotel, or a beanery. She liked his ideas and suggested that perhaps they could do it together.

"It's an idea," he'd said, but didn't commit himself. It was all so sudden. He felt as if he were being crowded into a corner. He had been free as the wind all these years. He wasn't sure exactly what he really wanted to do just yet. He needed time to think it over.

"You remind me of him, Jesse," Candy had told him.

"What, my ugly face?"

"The way you stand, tall and stooped over with that lazy, I don't give a damn look. Like you didn't have a care in the world. The sideways smile, too. He was always smiling. And the hair, too."

She went on a long time telling him how much he reminded her of her late husband. He didn't mind. "You miss him, don't you?"

"Very much, yes."

"I'm leaving in the morning," he told her.

"Where to?"

"Bremer's Rock. I left my horse there."

"Why did you do that?"

"It's a long story."

"Tell me. I like long stories."

He told her about Mallory. When he was finished, she asked him if he was coming back to Ellis.

"Most likely not."

She looked at him with sadness in her eyes.

The coach suddenly lurched. Garnett sat up and rubbed his bloodshot eyes. His mouth was whiskey dry, and the daylight hurt his head. He felt as if his head were caught in a bear trap.

He squinted around at the passengers. There were the usual carpetbaggers, two of them, sitting on the rear bench alongside him. A middle-aged woman and a young girl who was with her sat facing Garnett and the two carpetbaggers. A young cowboy sat next to the girl and kept stealing glances at her out of the corner of his eye.

They made the trip to Jubilee Flats in good time, arriving at eleven in the morning. By then everyone was pretty well shaken up and dusty. They stayed the usual forty-five minutes and changed horses.

It was a little after noontime when they started out for Kingston's Corners. They pulled in at about three in the afternoon. There was another forty-five minute layover for rest and another change of horses. Then they headed for West Fork, a mere ten mile stretch to the southeast.

At West Fork, a man in a suit tied his horse next to the cowboy's horse and got on the stage. Garnett figured he might be a gambler. He sat next to the young cowboy, facing Garnett and the two carpetbaggers.

The next stop was Bremer's Rock, another ten miles southwest. They were about three miles out of West Fork when the man pulled a gun from an inside shoulder harness under his coat.

"Hands high! Make it quick!"

Everyone held their hands over their heads. The young cowboy took a cloth sack out of his jacket and began searching the pockets of the carpetbaggers. He found a good amount of money. "These carpetbaggers are loaded," he said with a pleased smiled on his face.

"Check out the old lady. Be sure you get the ring. It's worth a few bucks," the man said.

The cowboy took the woman's purse and rummaged through it. He found some bills and coins. He dropped them into the sack and gave her back her purse. He glanced at her wedding ring and then back at her. The woman shook her head as if begging him not to take it. She was crying.

"The ring won't come off," the young cowboy said.

"Check out the girl."

The young cowboy glanced at the young girl. Their eyes met for a moment and he looked away.

"She ain't got nothin'," the cowboy said.

"Damn, kid," the man replied angrily, "you ain't much help, are you?"

One of the carpetbaggers growled, "You're not going to get away with this, mister!" His face was red with rage.

"Shut your face," the man yelled, "or I'll drill your ass!" He looked over at Garnett. "See what the saddle bum's got, kid."

The cowboy looked at Garnett for a second then leaned over to search him. As the coach hit a bump in the road, the carpetbagger drew a derringer, and fired off a shot at the man. The rocking of the coach threw his aim off and he hit the kid high in the chest. The man saw what had happened and turned to shoot the carpetbagger.

Garnett yelled at him, "Drop it!"

"Like hell!" the man replied.

Turning toward Garnett, the man thumbed off a shot as the stagecoach jerked again. His bullet missed Garnett's left arm by the width of a hair. Garnett's return shot hit the man in the chest, slamming his body against the backboard. He bounced forward and fell onto the floor of the coach.

The small coach skidded to a stop with brakes squealing. "What the heck's goin' on back there, Garnett?" Ben Stewart yelled.

"We had a holdup, Ben!"

The young shotgun jumped down, threw the door open and looked into the coach with his rifle at the ready. Everyone was holding their ears in pain and Garnett was shaking his head to clear it. The man's body fell halfway out of the coach door and lay there with his arms hanging down.

"Jesus!" the shotgun said.

Garnett got his boot against the man's body and shoved it the rest of the way out onto the road. He gently lifted the cowboy back over onto his seat, next to the girl. The young man slumped sideways against the side of the coach by the window.

"I'm sorry, Miss," he whispered softly to the girl. "I'm really sorry…"

The girl began to cry. The woman put her arms around her. The young cowboy started to say something more, but stopped. Blood bubbled from the corner of his mouth. He sighed as his chin fell on his chest. He didn't move anymore.

Garnett and the shotgun put the bodies of the two robbers in the back boot, and they continued on to Bremer's Rock. Stewart announced the forty-five- minute layover. He got two men who worked for the company to take care of the bodies.

"Looks like you got yourself another two horses, besides the two you already own from before," Stewart said.

"Yeah," Garnett replied. "Pretty soon I'll have a regular remuda."

Garnett hung around while Stewart made out a report. They went into the café to wait while the new team of horses were put in place. Finally, it was time to leave and the old passengers and the new ones got on the coach.

"Take it easy, Garnett," Stewart said.

"Yeah, and you do the same. Maybe I'll see you when you come back from Sterling. We'll have a drink together."

"Sure. That'll be good."

Garnett stood watching as the coach headed south for the next stop at Hood River. When the coach was out of sight, Garnett walked the two dead men's horses down to the stables where his big appaloosa and the other two outlaw horses were.

"Another two? You sure are a busy one," the stableman said with a chuckle.

"Yeah," Garnett said. "Horses just like ta follow me around, I guess."

"Yer pal Mallory sold off one of his horses and took the other one to go get the girl."

"What girl?"

"The one ol' Harlan Preston had come in. The one that was on the coach when you and Mallory first came to Bremer's Rock. Remember her?"

"Oh, yeah, now that you mention it. You say Mallory went after her?"

"Yep."

"Why?"

"Well, the story is, Preston was keepin' her at the ranch against her wishes."

"Why would he do that?"

"Agin, the story is she was supposed to bear him a child, but she changed her mind about it."

Garnett didn't believe it. "What?"

"Yep! Like I said, ol' Preston was a-holdin' her agin her will. Wouldn't let her leave the Circle H."

"Christ! It sounds like some crazy story from one of those romance magazines."

"It ain't no story. It's real."

"How long ago did Mallory leave?"

"A day ago."

"And he hasn't come back?"

"Nope, not as far as I know."

Garnett didn't say anything for a while. He stared out past the road to the hills beyond the stagecoach station. "A day ago, you say?" Garnett asked. The stableman nodded. "Then something must have happened."

"Knowin' Preston, I'd say yer friend is in deep trouble. Worse than that, he's most likely hangin' from the end of a rope somewhere."

Garnett looked worried. "I'm gonna mosey around. It might take a while. If you can sell my four horses and all the gear, you can take thirty percent. Would you be interested?"

The stableman laughed. "I sure would. You got yerself a deal, sonny."

They shook hands. Garnett saddled up the appaloosa. The horse scolded him, then nuzzled him against the stable fence. Garnett chuckled. "I sure missed you, too, old pal." He scratched the animal behind the ears, patted its neck and then swung up into the saddle.

"Where you headed, Garnett?"

"I'm gonna find out what happened."

"Well, you'd best be careful. Preston is one mean hombre. He don't like strangers on his land."

"How do I get there?"

"I'll draw ya a map. It's one heck of a big spread. But, like I said, be careful."

In half an hour, Garnett had a map of the area and an explanation of what to watch out for to avoid trouble. "Let's hit it, old pal!" he said to the appaloosa.

They started out slowly but soon the big horse was stretching out and biting the wind.

Chapter 7

It was dark and they were about five miles from the Circle H Ranch house when the temperature dropped sharply. Mallory led the way with the reins of Michelle's horse held tightly in his right hand, using his left one to guide the horse. Every few hundred yards he looked back to see how she was doing. Sometimes he fell back alongside her.

"Are you alright, Michelle?" Mallory asked.

"I think so." She didn't sound very sure.

Mallory soon realized her thin coat wasn't suited for the weather. She was shivering from the cold, and they were moving too slow. There was only one thing to do so he reined his horse to a stop and dismounted. Lifting her out of her saddle, he set her on his. After that, he tied the reins of her horse to his saddle strap, swung up behind her and nudged his horse into a fast walk.

"This is much better," she said, settling back between his arms. "I like this."

"So do I."

They made better time this way as they rode through a stretch of towering pine trees. It went on for a mile then opened into a wide field where they saw cows clustered together to keep warm. That worried Mallory. There might be some cowboys on night duty nearby. They thought they saw one at the far end of the field. Mallory nudged his horse faster until they came up over a rise and down a bank to a fast running stream. It looked deep.

"Are we going to cross it?" Michelle asked. "I'm afraid of deep water."

"Not here," he replied. "We'll find a shallow place."

He turned the horses to the north and followed along the edge of the stream. It turned and twisted. Once it ran between two rock walls. They rode around it, hoping it would split in two or run itself down to a level the horses could manage. Finally, they came to a place where the stream ran over a bed of gravel and rocks that sparkled in the light of the half moon.

"This might be the best chance we'll get," Mallory said.

"Alright then," she replied, "let's try it."

Mallory turned his horse into the water. Its iron-shod hooves rang on the rocks with each step. The water wasn't very deep, but it splashed up against their feet and legs. It was ice cold.

Half way across, Mallory's horse slipped and fell sideways, tossing them both into the frigid water. They stood up, gasping from the cold. Michelle had lost her purse. Mallory picked her up in his arms and rushed her toward the other side. When they got up on dry land, he set her down and looked back at the horses.

Michelle's horse broke loose and was running back in the opposite direction. Soon it was out of sight. Mallory's horse was screaming in pain trying to get up. Its left hind leg was broken at the lower joint and bone was showing.

Michelle began to cry, her sobs mixing with the screaming of the horse. Mallory walked back out into the icy water, grabbed the animal's reins and pulled, helping it stagger along on three legs. When they finally got to dry ground, he took the canteen, saddlebags, and the bedroll off the horse.

"Don't look," he said. She turned away as he shot the horse behind its right ear.

They were both wet. Michelle was shaking so hard her teeth chattered. He had to find a place to build a fire. "Come on," he said. "We're going to move fast to get the circulation going or else you'll get sick."

He started walking fast and she tried to keep up. After a little while, she began to tire. "I'm sorry, I can't."

"It's alright," he said and swept her up in his arms. He chuckled. "This will get my blood going."

Up ahead, about a hundred yards, Mallory saw a pile of boulders. As they got closer, he saw a small opening inside, a hidden pocket away from the wind. He set Michelle on her feet inside and gathered up some scattered branches and twigs.

He checked the top pocket of his shirt, inside his vest and coat. It was dry. He mixed some cigarette papers in with the twigs and touched a match to them. They burst into flames. While Michelle huddled around the fire, he squeezed the blanket as dry as he could and laid it across a boulder by the fire.

They sat as close to the flames as they could in an effort to dry their clothes. It took a while but they were eventually dry enough to be comfortable. They ate soggy beef jerky, damp hardtack and washed it down with water.

"A hot cup of coffee would be nice now, wouldn't it?" Michelle said, forcing a smile.

"It sure would," Mallory said. He took the blanket off the rock. It was dry and warm and he wrapped it around her. Then he leaned against the rock, soaking up the warmth.

Near dawn, they awoke to the sound of hound dogs barking on the far side of the stream. They grabbed up the blanket and saddlebags, and started walking quickly away. They headed to the east. The sun came out and it began to get warmer. Crossing a field of rocks, they moved between them like dancers. After a while, they couldn't hear the dogs anymore so they slowed down. Finally, they stopped to eat jerky and drink again, then walked on.

"Where are we, Kip?"

"I don't know. But if we keep going east I'm sure we'll hit the coach road."

"How far?"

"It can't be far," he said, not believing his own words. He said it just to keep her hope alive. But if they did get to the coach road, there was a chance of finding a town and help. He had plenty of money for another horse and saddle.

Michelle began to tire, and he picked her up again. "Don't," she said. "You'll hurt yourself."

He chuckled. "What? You're light as a feather."

They heard the hounds again, far away, just as a mass of dark clouds came blotting out the sun. The mass widened and deepened until it started to drop rain on them. It got very cold and they could see their breath come out in vapors.

Suddenly Mallory stumbled on a hidden rock and fell with her in his arms. They hit the ground hard and went rolling. Finally, they sat up, looking dazed.

"Are you alright?" he asked.

"My shoulder hurts a little but I'm fine."

They stood up and looked at each other. They were both covered with mud.

"Why are you bothering with me?" she asked.

"It seemed the right thing to do."

"Is that the only reason?"

"No. I guess you got to me like no other woman ever could."

"I'm sorry."

"For what?"

"For making you love me, if you do love me."

"It's that crazy little mouth of yours that did it, darlin'. And the way you smile. Your voice. Your eyes."

"Anything else?" She forced a laugh.

"I'll think of something when we're in a restaurant in Ellis," Mallory chuckled.

Michelle smiled. It started to rain harder. Mallory walked over to her and reached to pick her up.

"You're too tired. We'll walk," she told him.

They heard the hounds again. This time they were much closer.

Chapter 8

It was late morning on a cold day when Harlan Preston's buckboard pulled into the yard of the Circle H Ranch. He was tired and in a bad mood. His negotiations with the railroad men had gone sour. They wanted ten percent more to ship his cattle from Ellis to the Kansas City stockyards. On top of that, beef prices were falling, and there was no telling how far down they would go.

All around, Preston's financial situation wasn't good. He went into the study in the ranch house and tried to do some paperwork. He was about to call out for Michelle when his ramrod Whitmore came in and told him she was gone.

"Gone? What do you mean she's gone? I gave strict orders that she wasn't to leave the house."

"I know, but she got away, Mr. Preston."

"What happened, Whitmore?"

Cal Whitmore, the ramrod of the Circle H, was a big, hulking cowboy with a face only a mother could love, if she was half blind. In spite of his looks, he was a fair man. "We ain't figured it out jest yet, boss." Whitmore's voice was deep and crusty. It sounded as if he'd swallowed a bass drum. "As far as I kin see, some guy came an' took her."

"Took her? Against her will?"

"It ain't likely since she didn't do no screamin' fer help, accordin' to the old lady. They ran past her on the way out the back door."

"It was just one man? Just one?" Preston asked. He gritted his teeth until the muscles in his jaws bulged and rippled.

"Yep. Jest one, boss," Whitmore replied sheepishly. When his boss got mad, he could get nasty. The big ramrod had to choose his words carefully trying to avoid a blast of anger.

Preston grunted and nodded. His mind began to assess the matter. One person meant she had a lover, and this made Preston boiling mad. He recalled how it had happened before and swore it would never happen again. Now it had happened, and the cowboys would snicker and sneer behind his back. The story would get back to Bremer's Rock and each time he went to town they would laugh behind his back, knowing he was a betrayed man.

"How long have they been gone?" Preston asked.

"Two days now," Whitmore replied.

Preston sighed in resignation. "They're probably in Bremer's Rock by now."

"No sir, they ain't. I got three bloodhounds and five men on their trail. They're runnin' scared in the east quarter section right now. It won't be long before we get 'em."

Preston perked up and smiled. This was good news. She was still within his grasp. When he got her, he would come down on her like the hammers of hell. She was as good as dead already. And as for that man, whoever he was, he would suffer a slow, painful death.

"Good work, Whitmore! When you catch them, let me know. And don't bring them in. Take them over to the east line shack."

Whitmore's face clouded over. He knew what that meant, and he didn't know if he liked it or not. He knew what Harlan Preston could do, how mean he could be. It wasn't a cowboy's way to treat a woman like that.

"Alright, Mr. Preston," Whitmore said and left for the bunkhouse.

He was glad to get out of Preston's sight. Of late, the two hadn't been getting on too well. After only a year at the Circle H Ranch, Whitmore had heard stories and seen things that went against his grain. He didn't know how much longer he could tolerate Preston's brutal ways, his violating the cowboy code. He wasn't young anymore and Preston paid him top wages, so he went along, hating himself each day for doing so.

Up at the ranch house, Preston sighed and sat down. He grabbed a bottle of whiskey and a shot glass from the bottom drawer of his desk and poured himself a drink. Then he took a ledger and some documents from the top drawer, and started going over them.

The old woman, Maria, came in with a tray of food. He looked at the bacon, eggs, grits and coffee, and scowled.

"Take it away, old lady! I'm not hungry!"

Ignoring his words, she set it on the desk in front of him and left. He stared at it for a moment then started to nibble around the edges. Soon he was eating as he slowly went over the papers. However, just the thought of Michelle Logan running away with another man kept him from fully concentrating on the documents. He would not let her get away with cuckolding him like a common cowboy. She would come to feel his pain and much more. When he caught Michelle Logan and her lover, they would get a dose of Circle H justice.

Preston suddenly let out an anguished scream and sent the tray of food flying across the room. He heard footsteps. "Hey, boss!" Preston looked up. Whitmore was standing in the doorway all alone, staring at him. "They found them, boss!"

Preston got on his feet, trying to appear calm. He took a cigar from his vest and lit it. Logan saw that his hands trembled. "What's he like? The man she ran away with?"

"A tinhorn gambler. A nobody." That hurt even more. She had low taste in men. She had thrown him aside for a common piece of scum.

"Is he young?"

"Yeah. About her age, boss."

Preston's face clouded over and he nodded. "Where are they?"

"They're being taken to the east line shack. They should be there soon."

"Good. Have one of the boys get a can of lamp oil. We'll go pay them a visit."

"Lamp oil, boss?" Whitmore asked. He had heard well enough, but didn't like what he had heard. This was going to be bad for the girl. Very bad. He had heard rumors of the killing and the burning. It had happened long before he signed on.

"Yes, dammit! I said lamp oil!" The rancher's eyes looked like two blazing red coals from hell and his nostrils flared as he breathed hard. His face was flushed red with emotion and the veins bulged in his neck and forehead.

"Sure, boss," Whitmore said, "lamp oil."

"Have someone saddle my horse. I'll ride out and meet you at the east line shack as soon as I take care of some things."

Whitmore nodded and left. He went down to the bunkhouse to talk to the cowboy who had just rode in with the news, the same one who had just brought the bloodhounds back. They had done their job well.

"Tim, I want ya ta get a can of lamp oil and take it back out ta the east line shack."

"Who says?"

"The boss. He'll be out there soon."

"Christ! I jest came in!"

"I know."

"Is he goin' crazy?"

Whitmore sighed and looked away for a moment, then nodded. "I don't know. Maybe he's been crazy all along and we jest never noticed."

Tim knew better than to argue with the big ramrod. In half an hour, he mounted up and headed out for the east line shack with a gallon can of lamp oil in one hand. He never noticed a lone rider on a black and white appaloosa was shadowing him.

Chapter 9

Jesse Garnett could see the cowboy fifty yards ahead riding at a slow lope. The man had his left hand on his horse's reins while he rode with the other holding the handle of a galvanized can. It had a pouring spout, was painted bright red and was very easy to see against the trunks of the bare trees.

They had been on the trail for well over an hour when the cowboy turned left and rode down into a gully. A line shack was there, next to a stream. Garnett stopped and watched.

As the cowboy rode up to the shack two men came out. He handed one of them the can, then dismounted. They talked a while and finally went into the shack.

Garnett dismounted and walked his horse around to the blind side of the shack into a cluster of scrub oaks. He tied his horse there, walked slowly over to the windowless side of the shack and put his ear against the wall. He could barely hear the voices inside because of the wind. He waited patiently. Finally, it died down.

One voice sounded like it came from Kip Mallory. He was arguing with someone. There was a thud of a fist against flesh. Mallory groaned in pain. Garnett walked quickly around to the front of the shack. He grabbed a lariat off one of the horses tied to the rail and opened the line shack door. One of the three men noticed him and stepped outside to confront him. He was the one with the galvanized can.

"Who the hell are you, fellah?"

Garnett slapped him alongside the head with the butt of his Colt, knocking him senseless to the ground. Then he stepped into the shack with his gun at the ready.

"Don't try it!" Garnett growled as the taller of the two men inside made a move for his gun. The man froze. Garnett glanced at the shorter one and said, "Untie them and make it quick."

"I'm sure glad to see you, pard," Mallory said when he was loose. Garnett saw that his lips were swollen, and that his face was bruised. "How'd you find us?"

"We'll talk later," Garnett said. "It's time to go. Others are coming." He tossed the lasso to Mallory.

Mallory stood the two cowboys back to back, wound the entire length of rope around their bodies and shoved them down on a bunk.

"We have to hurry," Garnett warned.

He looked at Michelle and recognized her as the woman on the stagecoach. He gave her a nod of recognition as Mallory untied her.

"It seems you're always helping me, Mr. Garnett."

"My pleasure, ma'am."

Mallory looked around for his gun, found it and shoved it into his holster. Picking Michelle up, he carried her outside, put her on one of the cowboys' horses, then climbed up behind her. Garnett mounted the big appaloosa. They heard horses in the woods about a hundred yards away.

"We gotta go!" Garnett said.

"I'm right behind you, pal!" Mallory replied.

They started at a gallop, cutting into a stand of pines with Garnett leading. He glanced up at the sun to get his bearing and saw they were heading north. Turning his horse to the right, he steered them east through the trees. In no time, the pines were behind them and they struck out across an open field of buffalo grass. When they reached the far side, they heard horses behind them. Michelle glanced back.

"It's him!" she screamed. "Oh God!"

Grasping the reins in his left hand, Mallory twisted around in the saddle and thumbed off several shots at the group of riders coming hard upon them. He saw Garnett head the appaloosa into a grove of birch trees at the far edge of the field and followed him in.

They had to slow down again as they rode twisting and swerving to avoid the tree branches and trunks. At the end of the grove, the land dropped sharply downward into a long slope. The horses balked.

"This looks bad!" Mallory cried out. Michelle saw the sheer drop and moaned.

"Come on, pal!" Garnett yelled at the appaloosa. "Show 'em what you got, pal!" He urged the big horse over the edge.

The ground was soft, and both man and horse went sliding down the slope with the big appaloosa's rump scraping the ground. Halfway down, the horse completely lost its footing, spun around, and began traveling along on its side. Both man and beast went sailing along, plowing up the loose earth. Garnett finally got loose of the stirrups, jumped off and slid to a stop. He sat on the slope and watched the appaloosa finally hit the bottom. It struggled to get to its feet, shook itself and looked back up at him as if to ask, "What the hell was that all about?"

Mallory's horse soon slid past Garnett, its saddle empty. He looked back to see Mallory and Michelle sliding down towards him on their backsides. They stopped nearby and sat there a moment before standing up, and scrambling the rest of the way down the slope. Garnett got to his feet and followed. At the bottom, as they checked the horses, they heard noise above and looked up to see Preston and his men.

"Let's go!" Mallory yelled.

"I'll take her," Garnett said.

"Alright!" Mallory replied. He thrust Michelle up behind Garnett's cantle saying, "Hold on, little darling!" She wrapped her arms around Garnett's waist and they rode off. Mallory fired two more shots up at the top of the slope then urged his horse into a gallop. He soon caught up with the appaloosa.

"You okay, ma'am?" Garnett yelled back to Michelle as they rode along.

"Yes. I'm fine!"

"Then, hold tight!"

The appaloosa stretched out with long strides and the cold wind flew past them. Mallory got his mount to step it up and they were soon riding side by side across a long, flat stretch of barren land that led between high hills topped with pines. A thousand yards ahead, it came to a dead end. The only way out was up the steep sides.

They hit the bottom of the hill at breakneck speed and plunged upward. By the time they were halfway, the horses began to slow down. Garnett glanced down. He counted eight riders coming across the open area below. Preston was behind the others, but not far back.

After what seemed an eternity, the appaloosa and the mustang struggled up on level ground. They stood gasping for air, exhausted and spent.

Garnett patted the big horse's neck. "Good boy."

Mallory reloaded his gun and thumbed two more shots down at the riders below. They stopped to look up.

Preston shook his fist at them. "I'll get you, girl!" he bellowed at the top of his lungs. "I'll get you and that piece of scum with you!"

"Let's get out of here," Mallory yelled, still breathing hard. The horses were winded and barely moved at a fast walk.

"They need water," Garnett said. They moved slowly across the hill, through a stand of pines and into the open again, where they stopped to look. A gentle slope led downward.

"Look," Mallory shouted, pointing off into the distance.

There was a small stream down below. It sparkled as it meandered alongside a road. A tall cottonwood stood nearby, between the stream and the road. Its leaves were turning yellow. Many of its limbs were bare. A blanket of yellow and brown leaves lay around its base.

Garnett knew where they were. "That's the coach road!" he yelled.

The horses smelled the water and moved quickly down the gentle slope through the broom sedge. Once they were across the road, they hurried to the stream to drink.

"Here they come!" Mallory said, pointing back to where the Circle H cowboys were riding down the slope towards them. "We're in for it now, pard!"

Garnett said, "Maybe we can bluff our way out."

They watched as Preston and his eight men rode hard across the road and up to the stream. They fanned out, forming a half circle. The rancher was out front, in the middle.

"Is he the one?" Preston asked, pointing at Garnett and Michelle.

"No, it's the other one," one of the cowboys replied, pointing out Mallory.

The rancher scrutinized Mallory closely with a crooked sneer on his mouth. "I'll tend to you later, mister," he growled. He turned to Garnett and Michelle and moved his horse closer to them. He stared at her, then Garnett.

"Who the hell are you?" he asked Garnett with a scowl.

"Garnett. Jesse Garnett."

"Well, Jesse Garnett, what the hell are you doing with my woman?"

The Circle H cowboys looked on with curious interest, especially the ramrod, Whitmore, who seemed concerned.

"Do you have papers on her?" Garnett asked.

It was an unexpected and logical question, and the Circle H cowboys understood the implication. It referred to legal ownership of property. In the case of a woman, it was a lawful document, a marriage license. The asking of it set Preston back on his heels. He didn't like his authority being put to the test.

"If I say she's mine then she's mine and that's the end of it! Who the hell are you to question me?"

Garnett shrugged. He hesitated for a moment, and then dismounted. He helped Michelle down on the ground.

"Ma'am, would you mind going over there by Mr. Mallory and wait?"

Mallory dismounted and Michelle walked quickly over to him. He put an arm around her, holding her close. They both stared apprehensively at Garnett, wondering what was coming next. Garnett looked around at the Circle H cowboys.

Judging from the looks on their faces, they weren't happy. Before them stood a pair of young lovers whose fate was in their hands. The Circle H cowboys sat in their saddles looking down, avoiding Michelle's pleading stare, ashamed of what they were about to do.

Preston's face was red with anger and his eyes narrowed. He pointed a finger at Garnett.

"Whitmore, I seem to be having a problem here. I'd like it if you or one of your men took care of this saddle tramp. Do it quickly, please. I want him out of the way so we can take care of the business at hand."

Whitmore looked over at Garnett and then at his men. There was a look of indecision on his face. He wasn't sure he wanted to comply with Preston's demand. He fully understood what the business at hand was going to be. Finally, he asked, "Any you boys wanna do it?" He waited. No one moved or spoke up.

When the rancher realized that no one was about to brace Garnett, he said quickly, "I'll give a hundred dollars to anyone who puts a bullet in this fool."

The Circle H cowboys glanced at each other with concerned looks. No one moved. It was a few moments before someone said, "Hell, for a hundred, I'll do it!"

A tall, lean cowboy wearing his black hat low and chewing on a matchstick climbed slowly down from his horse, then walked over to a clear spot away from the others. He turned to face Garnett with a casual smile on his lips, his hand down by his gun, his legs braced. He took the matchstick from his mouth and let it fall onto the ground.

"Thank you, Cramer," Preston said. "Make it quick and clean, won't you?"

"My pleasure, sir," Cramer replied. "Where do you want the bullet, Mr. Preston?"

"Between his eyes, for two hundred."

"Sure," Cramer replied, "I'll do that fer you, sir."

Whitmore looked over at the cowboy. "You sure, Cramer?" Whitmore asked. "You jest joined up. You wanna die before yer first month's pay?"

Cramer sneered at Garnett. "Hell, he ain't nothin'. I've seen his kind before. They're all wind and no sand." He stood staring at Garnett with an eager look on his face. He wanted that two hundred dollars bad.

"You ready, saddle bum?" Cramer shouted.

Garnett never answered. His hand became a blur as he fanned off two shots. One hit Cramer in the chest and the other hit him between the eyes. His body jerked and spun in a complete circle before it collapsed alongside the road in a twisted heap.

"Yeah, I'm ready," Garnett said, finally answering Cramer's question.

Mallory already had his gun out pointing in the direction of the Circle H cowboys. They were caught in the saddle and bunched up. It was a bad place to be. They kept their hands in view. It was like a game of chess. Positions could be an advantage.

Preston looked over at his ramrod. He looked less confident now, a little frightened.

"I guess you'll have to take care of this problem, then, Mr. Whitmore. Please do so now, so we can settle the matter. There's a gallon of lamp oil waiting at the east line shack to be put to use."

"Why don't you take care of it, Preston, seeing as it's your problem and nobody else's?" Garnett said.

Preston pretended not to hear Garnett. "Did you hear me, Whitmore?"

"Yeah, I heard you, Mr. Preston," Whitmore said. "An' you kin take that lamp oil an' set yerself on fire, for all I care!"

Preston was stunned. He had always gotten his way. Money and his misuse of authority had seen to that. Now his ramrod had turned on him. The grip he once had seemed to be slipping fast. He looked around for someone to blame besides himself, someone to turn his rage on. A scapegoat. He glared at Michelle.

"This is all your fault, girl! After all that I've done for you, you stab me in the back! Well, you're not going to cuckold me and get away with it!"

Preston drew. Mallory saw him, but couldn't take a shot because Michelle was in the way. As he shoved her away, Preston fired and hit her high on the right side. Michelle sank down on her knees, staring up at Mallory.

"Kip!" she groaned.

Mallory dropped his gun and grabbed her to keep her from hitting the ground.

"Oh, God!" he moaned.

Preston took aim again. Garnett couldn't get a clean shot at him because one of the cowboys was in the way. Whitmore reached over, and knocked the gun out of Preston's hand. The rancher glared fiercely at him.

"You're finished, Whitmore!" He screamed, looking around. "You're all done for! I got no use for yellow bellies like you! You're all finished! Get out of my sight! All of you!"

The cowboys of the Circle H didn't move. They sat there staring at Mallory as he held Michelle in his arms. They couldn't look away. One of them rode over alongside Mallory and asked if he could do anything. Mallory shook his head. "It's too late, she's gone," he muttered. "She's gone."

The cowboy looked over at Whitmore and said, "We can't let this stand, boss. We gotta vote. It's the code."

Whitmore nodded. He turned to the Circle H cowboys. "He's right, men. We gotta take care of this an' right now."

He glanced at where Mallory rocked Michelle in his arms, sobbing. "We'll take a vote. Who votes fer the code?"

They all raised their hands. When Preston saw it, he tried turning his horse to make a run for it, but couldn't. They had him boxed in.

Whitmore growled, "Take him, boys!"

The Circle H cowboys dismounted, grabbed Preston and yanked him out of the saddle. He yelled and struggled to get away but they held him fast. Whitmore pointed to the big cottonwood. They hoisted Preston high in the air and carried him over to it. He screamed and kicked all the way. Garnett and Mallory watched, not believing their eyes. They were about to see cowboy justice for Michelle Logan.

When they got to the cottonwood, one of the cowboys tossed a rope over a high, stout branch. Whitmore placed the noose around Preston's neck. Altogether, they grabbed the rope and pulled him up into the tree.

"Higher," Whitmore said. "We don't want the coyotes eatin' on him. He's pure poison."

They left Preston dangling ten feet above the ground and went back to stand by their horses.

"We're sorry about this, Mallory," Whitmore said. "Really sorry."

The ramrod motioned to his cowboys and swung up into the saddle. They stood with a sad look on their faces for a moment then mounted up with him.

Whitmore glanced over at Garnett. "You never saw us, Garnett. Okay?"

Garnett nodded back. "I never saw you, Whitmore. Good luck."

All the cowboys removed their hats in a solemn salute to Michelle Logan, then rode away from the Circle H Ranch. Garnett and Mallory watched them go.

When they were out of sight, Garnett turned to Mallory. He was holding Michelle's limp body in his arms, rocking her back and forth, as he cried. Garnett stood silently aside and waited.

Finally, Mallory looked up, his eyes flooded with tears. "Help me, Jesse. We can't leave her here."

"We won't, Kip. We'll take care of her."

Just then, they heard horses on the coach road coming from the northeast. In a few minutes, the six horse Branford

& Smith cargo wagon came into view. Garnett raised his arms and stepped out into the road to block it. It came to a screeching halt five feet in front of him, its brakes smoking.

"Move aside or I'll plug you!" the shotgun said.

"I'm Jesse Garnett. I'm a friend of Ben Stewart. We need your help."

"Any friend of Ben Stewart is a friend of mine," the whip hollered out. He saw Preston's hanging corpse and Michelle Logan's body. "What in God's name happened here?"

After Garnett told him the story, the whip said, "Put her on the wagon and we'll take her into Bremer's Rock."

They wrapped Michelle's body in a blanket from Mallory's bedroll, and placed it on the back of the flat-bottomed wagon. Mallory climbed up and lay down alongside her. The cargo wagon moved slowly out for Bremer's Rock, five miles away.

Garnett gave Preston's body a last glance. A large crow had landed on his shoulder. It began cawing to its clan. Two came and then more, landing on Preston's head and wherever they could get a foothold. Garnett turned away and fell in behind the wagon with Mallory's horse tied to his saddle strap.

Chapter 10

Mallory and Garnett arranged to have a proper service and burial for Michelle at the little church in Bremer's Rock. After the ceremony, they put her pinewood casket in the back of a buckboard belonging to the church and took it up to the graveyard on the hill at the edge of town.

The pastor and a few people from his parish attended the funeral. A woman and her daughter sang "Amazing Grace" and the pastor read several verses from the Old Testament. There were no flowers on the grave. It was too cold for flowers, but someone had thought to bring a sprig of mistletoe.

After the short ceremony was over and everyone had left, Garnett stayed to talk to Mallory. It seemed right to do so. They would be saying goodbye soon, and Garnett never liked saying goodbye. He and Mallory had been through a lot together. There was a bond of brotherhood between them, even though he was a drifter and Mallory was a gambler, and even though their lifestyles were very different from each other. They had mutual respect and that was all that mattered.

It was a cold, blustery afternoon and the tops of the nearby pines trees swayed in the wind. Mallory imagined they were whispering Michelle's name repeatedly. Michelle…Michelle…Michelle… He was finished with crying now. Michelle's death had taken a lot out of him. There was nothing left to do, but talk to his friend Garnett.

"I was going to take her to California with me," Mallory said. "She was always cold. She would have liked the warm weather there." Garnett smiled sadly at his friend and nodded. Suddenly Mallory blurted out, "Heck, it never would have worked out, me being a gambler."

"You never know," Garnett replied. "But I guess you're probably right, when you think about it."

"Yeah. It probably never would have worked out. I'd get the itch to move on and she'd want to settle down and have kids. It wouldn't have worked."

Garnett knew his friend didn't believe his own words. His heart was broken, and it would be a long time before it healed. He had met a sweet girl and fallen in love with her, and now she was gone, taken away by a whim of fate.

Garnett finally stepped back, put his hat on and took a last look at Michelle's grave. "I'll give you some time," he said.

"Thanks," Mallory replied, choking up.

Garnett walked slowly out of the graveyard and down the bank to the road. He went to the appaloosa and stood rubbing its neck and ears. The big horse whinnied and pressed its head against him as if trying to comfort him. A few minutes later Mallory came down, wiping the tears from his eyes.

"The Pastor said he'd take care of the grave. I gave him some money. I'll send more when I get to where I'm going," the gambler said.

"Sure," was all Garnett could think of saying. He was at a loss for words.

Mallory sighed. "Well, Garnett, it's been great riding with you."

"Where are you headed, Kip?"

"I haven't decided. Maybe I'll mosey on up to Ellis and take the train to San Francisco. I heard the gambling is good there,"

A cold wind blew down from the graveyard, bringing with it the feel of winter.

"Yeah, that sounds like a good idea. It'll be snowing here soon," Garnett replied.

"Yeah, that's what I'm thinking, too," Mallory said. He paused to stare back up the hill to the graveyard. Finally, he turned back to Garnett. "How about you? Got anything special in mind?"

"No, nothing special," Garnett replied. He wanted to see Candy Clarkson again, but he didn't want to say it outright. After all, his friend just lost his sweetheart and was in mourning.

There didn't seem to be anything more to say so they shook hands and mounted up. Mallory saluted Garnett, turned his horse and rode away. Garnett watched him until the gambler came to a bend in the road. Mallory stopped, turned in the saddle, waved again and rode out of sight.

A blast of cold air came from the north again and shook the trees along the road, blowing off the last of the dead leaves. Garnett looked around, suddenly realizing he was all alone. A dog barked somewhere behind a building nearby.

Garnett looked up at the low, gray clouds then shivered and pulled his coat collar higher.

He clicked his tongue at the appaloosa, and they moved along the road towards the west side of town, in the direction of the stagecoach stop. He soon saw the warm lights in the windows of the Branford & Smith way station. As he moved closer, he caught the mouthwatering smell of hot food and coffee. He could also hear the voices of people coming from the dining room. Tying up at the rail, Garnett walked in through the foyer where people sat on benches waiting for the next stage to arrive. A sign on the wall indicated a stage from Ellis was due at six in the evening.

The dining room was warm, cozy and well lit. Garnett sat down at a table, ordered coffee and rolled a cigarette. When the coffee came, he paid, put out the cigarette and took a drink. It was hot and bitter, just the way he liked it. As he sat sipping coffee, he looked around. There were perhaps a dozen people in the place. Some were eating while others were drinking. Some were most likely just waiting to be picked up by friends or family.

Suddenly Garnett felt very lonely. He watched the people interacting with each other, touching hands, stroking cheeks, talking, kissing and laughing. He thought about Mallory out on the road in the cold, and of Michelle in the grave up on the hill, and he felt a deep sadness for them both. Then he thought about Candy Clarkson, and it hit him hard that he had turned down a chance to grab onto a normal life. A life like the people sitting around him were having.

He stood up and walked quickly outside to the porch. He had to go back to her, to Ellis, eighty miles north. He had to see her, to hold her again. He had been a fool to turn her down. Maybe it was too late now, but he had to take a chance. Swinging up into the saddle, he turned his horse onto the coach road and nudged it into a gentle run.

About five miles north of the Bremer's Rock he saw the southbound Branford & Smith stagecoach coming towards him. He moved off the road to get out of its way. As it sped past, he heard someone call out his name. For a moment Garnett thought it was his imagination, but then he saw a woman's hand wave at him from the coach window. He quickly turned the appaloosa and followed along behind it.

As the coach came to a stop at the way station, Garnett rode up alongside, slid from the saddle and ran to the door. It flew open, and Candy Clarkson came rushing out at him. Her arms wrapped tightly around Garnett's neck as she hugged him. He held her close, not knowing if this was really happening, if she was there or not. Her lips told him she was. The passengers walked by smiling and hooting, at the couple, as they went into the station.

"I was just going up to Ellis to see you about that offer you made," Garnett said. "The one about going into business?"

"Well, what's your answer, Jesse?"

"My answer is yes, little darling. I'm ready."

"That's what I wanted to hear, love. Now let's go home," Candy replied.

Garnett looked up at the darkening sky and said, "Thank you, Lord."

It began to snow. Up on the driver's bench, Ben Stewart called down to him, "How's this fer service, pal?"

Garnett waved but didn't answer. He was busy taking care of business. Jesse Garnett had finally gone to roost.

The End

Western books by R. Annan

Fight for the Lazy M
The Red Bandana
The Salvation of Trace Logan
The Cowboy from Sierra Blanca

Jack Cordell Westerns

The Gunfighter in Winter
Long Ride to Hell's Kitchen
Owl Hawks
Gunfight at Barfield Springs
Shootout at Sanctuary City
Last Days of a Gunfighter

Clay Jared Westerns

Copperhead Moon
Cowboys of the Box R
Prisoners of Brimstone Pass
Range War in C Minor
Devil Wind
Showdown at Wamego Falls
Lightning Riders
Winter Kill
Wild River
Shootout at Rattlesnake Flats

Jesse Garnett Westerns

Gunfight at Black Wolf Lair
Gunfight at Latigo Junction
Outcasts of Troublesome Creek
Stagecoach to Bremer's Rock

About the Author

As a young boy growing up in the city, R. Annan never passed up a chance to see a western movie. His heroes were Buck Jones, Johnny Mack Brown, Wild Bill Elliot and John Wayne, to name a few. As an adult, he often wondered where his love of westerns came from. Perhaps it has something to do with his grandfather, John L. Annan, who was a cowboy from Helena, Montana, in days of old.

R. Annan is a seasoned and traveled author with many interests. As a career serviceman, he served in Korea and Vietnam. He also completed a one-year course at the Defense Language Institute at Monterey, California, and graduated from the University of South Florida with a B.A. in Art and Art History. After taking a two-year course in screenwriting at the Hollywood Scriptwriting Institute, he established The Old Time Radio Club Time Machine as both a scriptwriter and an actor.

A Note from the Author

Thank you for reading my book. If you enjoyed it, would you please consider rating and reviewing it? I'd enjoy your feedback. Thank you!